FUN學美國[illegible]學科

Preschool 閱讀課本 二版

AMERiCAN SCHOOL TEXTBOOK

Reading Key

6

Preschool
數字篇

作者 ◎ Michael A. Putlack &
e-Creative Contents
譯者 ◎ 歐寶妮

Authors

Michael A. Putlack

Michael A. Putlack graduated from Tufts University in Medford, Massachusetts, USA, where he got his B.A. in History and English and his M.A. in History. He has written a number of books for children, teenagers, and adults.

e-Creative Contents

A creative group that develops English contents and products for ESL and EFL students.

The Best Preparation for Building Basic Vocabulary and Grammar

The Reading Key — Preschool series is designed to help children understand basic words and grammar to learn English. This series also helps children develop their reading skills in a fun and easy way.

Features

- Learning high-frequency words that appear in all kinds of reading material
- Building basic grammar and reading comprehension skills to learn English
- Various activities including reading and writing practice
- A wide variety of topics that cover American school subjects
- Full-color photographs and illustrations

The Reading Key series has five levels.

- Reading Key **Preschool 1–6**
  a six-book series designed for preschoolers and kindergarteners
- Reading Key **Basic 1–4**
  a four-book series designed for kindergarteners and beginners
- Reading Key **Volume 1–3**
  a three-book series designed for beginner to intermediate learners
- Reading Key **Volume 4–6**
  a three-book series designed for intermediate to high-intermediate learners
- Reading Key **Volume 7–9**
  a three-book series designed for high-intermediate learners

Table of Contents | Preschool 6 Numbers

Components Workbook for Daily Review • Answers and Translations

Syllabus | Preschool 6 Numbers

Subject	Unit	Grammar	Vocabulary
Basic Numbers Kids Need to Know	Unit 1 Numbers from 1 to 5	• Numbers from 1 to 5 • Numbers and common nouns	• one, two, three, four, five • dog, puppy, cat, kitten, goldfish, bird • I have/How many
	Unit 2 Numbers from 6 to 10	• Numbers from 6 to 10 • Numbers and common nouns	• six, seven, eight, nine, ten • birthday cake, candle, present • cup, cupcake, balloon • . . . years old
	Unit 3 One More, One Less	• Simple calculations	• ant, butterfly, ladybug, bee • plus, minus, equal • one more, one less
	Unit 4 Numbers from 11 to 20	• Numbers from 11 to 20 • Numbers and common nouns	• eleven, twelve, thirteen, fourteen, fifteen, sixteen, seventeen, eighteen, nineteen, twenty • animal, lion, tiger, elephant, insect
	Unit 5 Numbers from 10 to 100	• Numbers from 10 to 100 • Money	• ten, twenty, thirty, forty, fifty, sixty, seventy, eighty, ninety, one hundred • dollar, cent • How much is it?
	Unit 6 Numbers from 1st to 10th	• Numbers from 1st to 10th • Ordinal numbers	• first, second, third, fourth, fifth, sixth, seventh, eighth, ninth, tenth, last • alphabet, letter
	Unit 7 Time	• Reading time	• 1 o'clock – 12 o'clock • 1:30 (one thirty), 2:10 (two ten) • What time is it?
	Unit 8 Reading Calendars	• Reading calendars	• days, weeks, dates • year, month, day, hour

UNIT
1
Numbers from 1 to 5
01
Key Words Read the words.
1
one
2
two
3
three
4
four
5
five

dog

puppy

cat

kitten

goldfish

bird

Match the words with the pictures.

Let's Count

Circle the correct word for each picture.

There is (**one**, **two**) cat.

There are (**two**, **three**) kittens.

There is (**one**, **two**) dog.

There are (**two**, **three**) puppies.

There are (**three**, **four**) birds.

There are (**four**, **five**) goldfish.

I Have

Circle the words **in blue**.

I have two cats.

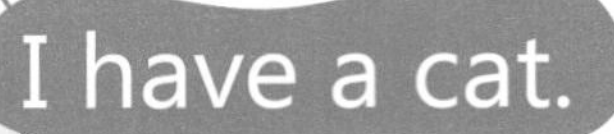

I have four dogs.

I have a dog.

I have three birds.

I have a bird.

I have five goldfish.

I have a goldfish.

Put a check under the correct picture.

 How many cats do you have?  I have five cats.

☐  ☑ 

 How many dogs do you have?  I have three dogs.

☐  ☐ 

 How many birds do you have?  I have two birds.

☐  ☐ 

 How many goldfish do you have?  I have two goldfish.

☐  ☐ 

I Can Read

Read the story.

Circle the correct word for each picture.

How Many Cats Are There?

How many cats are there?

There are (**two**, **three**) cats.

How many dogs are there?

There are (**two**, **three**) dogs.

How many birds are there?

There are (**four**, **five**) birds.

How many goldfish are there?

There are (**four**, **five**) goldfish.

UNIT
2
Numbers from 6 to 10
07
Key Words
Read the words.
six
seven
eight
nine
ten

present

candle

birthday cake

cup

cupcake

balloon

Match Up

Match the words with the pictures.

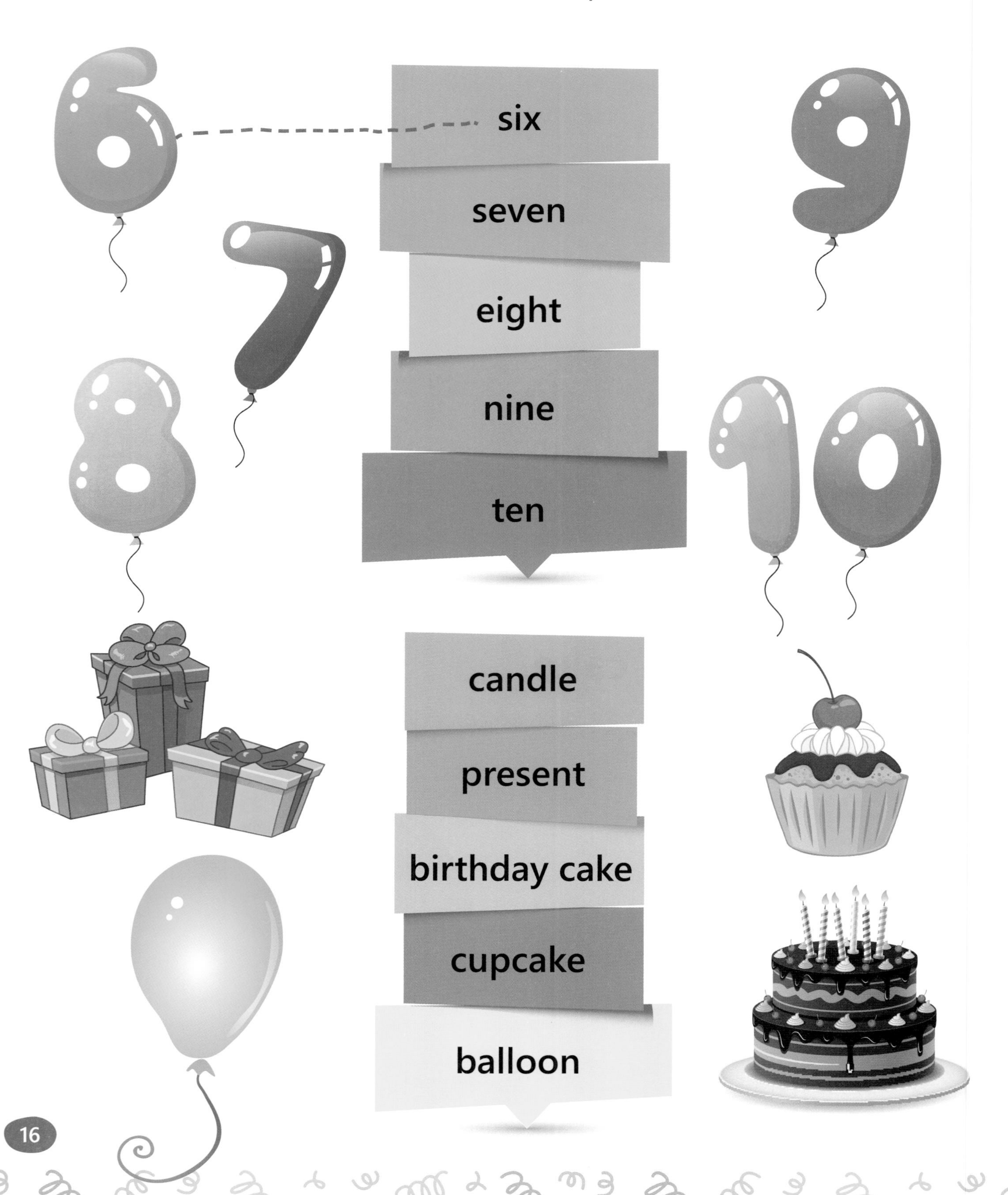

How Many?

Circle the correct word for each picture.

There are (six, seven) presents.

There are (**seven, eight**) candles.

There are (**eight, nine**) cups.

There are (**eight, nine**) cupcakes.

There are (**nine, ten**) balloons.

There Are

Circle the correct word for each sentence.

There are (six, **seven**) candles.
I am 6 years old.

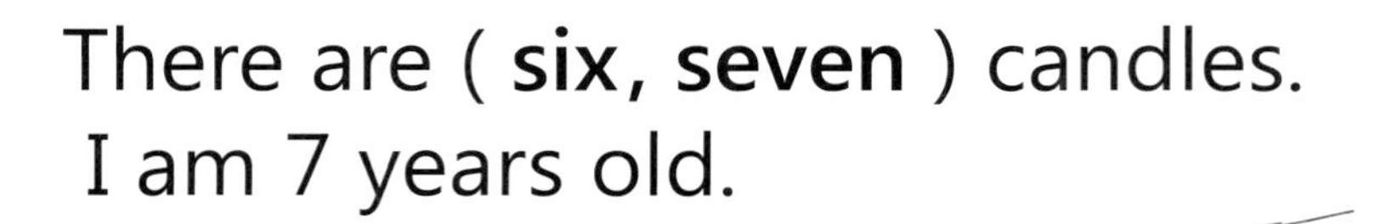

There are (**six, seven**) candles.
I am 7 years old.

There are (**seven, eight**) candles.
I am 8 years old.

There are (**eight, nine**) candles.
I am 9 years old.

There are (**nine, ten**) candles.
I am 10 years old.

How Old Are You?

Circle the correct word for each sentence.

How old are you?

I am (**nine**, **ten**) years old.

How old are you?

I am (**eight**, **nine**) years old.

How old are you?

I am (**seven**, **eight**) years old.

How old are you?

I am (**six**, **seven**) years old.

How old are you?

I am (**six**, **seven**) years old.

I Can Read

Read the story. Circle the words **in blue**.

Let's have a party.

There are six candles.
I am 6 years old.

How many candles are there?

There are seven candles.
I am 7 years old.

How many candles are there?

There are eight candles.
I am 8 years old.

How many candles are there?

There are ten candles.
I am 10 years old.

UNIT 3

One More, One Less

Key Words

13 Read the words.

three butterflies
five bees
two ants
four ladybugs
plus
minus
equal

Match Up

Match the words with the pictures.

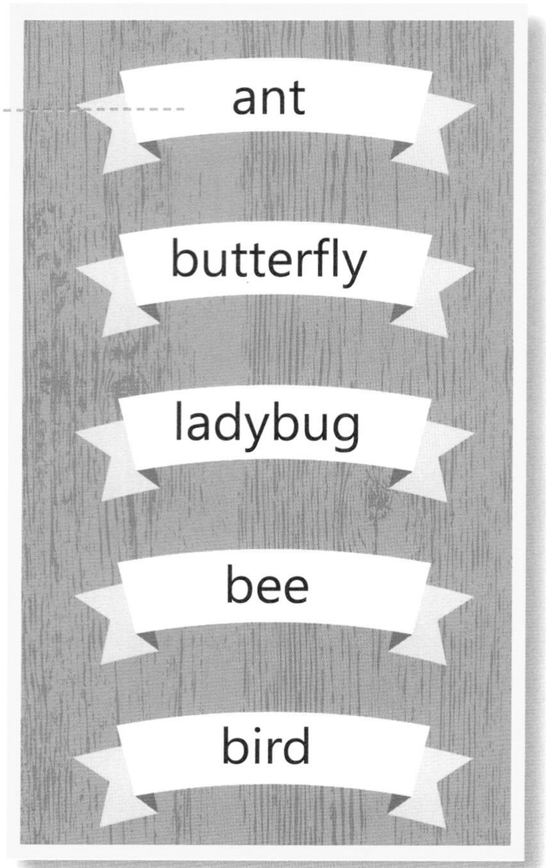

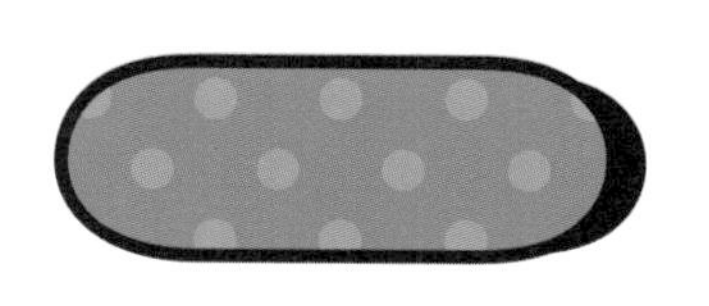

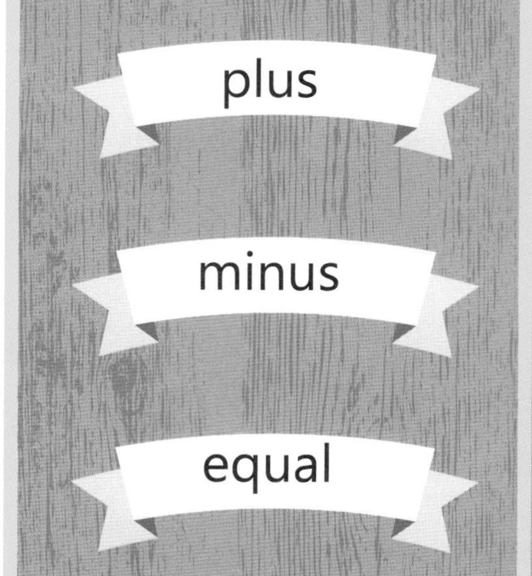

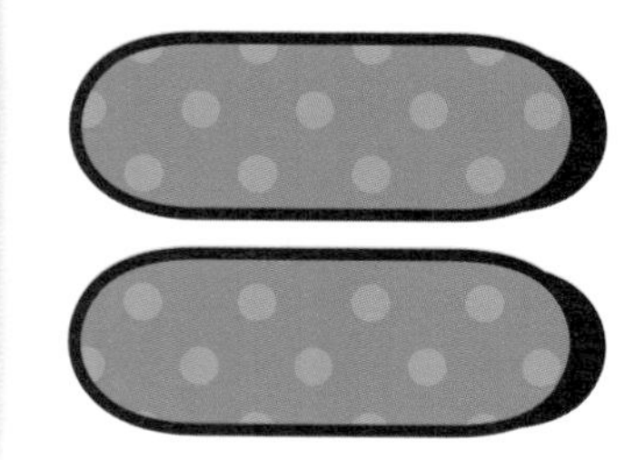

How Many?

Circle the correct word for each picture.

five bees + one bee = (six, seven) bees

six bees + one bee = (six, seven) bees

seven bees + one bee = (seven, eight) bees

eight bees − one bee = (seven, eight) bees

nine bees − one bee = (eight, nine) bees

One More, One Less

Circle the words **in blue**.

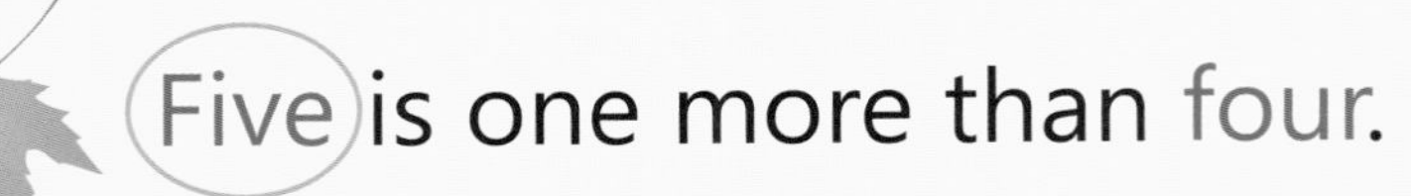
5 Five is one more than four. 4

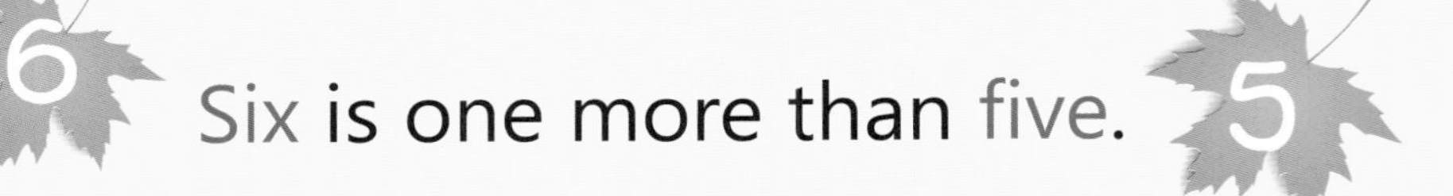
6 Six is one more than five. 5

7 Seven is one more than six. 6

7 Seven is one less than eight. 8

8 Eight is one less than nine. 9

One More or One Less?

Circle the correct word for each sentence.

I see six butterflies.

Six is (**one more**, **one less**) than five.

I see seven ladybugs.

Seven is (**one more, one less**) than six.

I see eight birds.

Eight is (**one more, one less**) than nine.

I see nine bees.

Nine is (**one more, one less**) than ten.

chant 18
I Can Read
Read the story. Circle the words in blue.
I see four butterflies.
Now there are five.
I see five ladybugs.
Now there are six.

Honey
I see six bees.
Now there are seven.
I see seven ants.
Now there are eight.

UNIT 4

Numbers from 11 to 20

Key Words

19 Read the words.

11 eleven
12 twelve
13 thirteen
14 fourteen
15 fifteen
16 sixteen
17 seventeen
18 eighteen
19 nineteen
20 twenty

animal

lion

elephant

tiger

insect

Match the words with the pictures.

How Many?

Circle the correct word for each picture.

six birds + seven birds = (13, 14) birds

three ants + eleven ants = (13, 14) ants

eight ladybugs + seven ladybugs = (15, 16) ladybugs

four bees + twelve bees = (16, 17) bees

How Many Animals Are There?

Circle the correct word for each sentence.

- There are three (**lion**, **lions**) in Row 1.
- There are four (**tiger**, **tigers**) in Row 2.
- There are five (**elephant**, **elephants**) in Row 3.
- There are (**eleven**, **twelve**) animals all together.

How Many Insects Are There?

Circle the correct word for each sentence.

How many bees are in Row 1?

There are (**five**, **six**) bees in Row 1.

How many ants are in Row 2?

There are (**six**, **seven**) ants in Row 2.

How many ladybugs are in Row 3?

There are (**seven**, **eight**) ladybugs in Row 3.

How many insects are there all together?

There are (**seventeen**, **eighteen**) insects all together.

I Can Read

Read the story.

Circle the correct number for each sentence.

Let's Count.

How many pencils are there?

There are (**eleven**, **twelve**) pencils.

How many balls are there?

There are (**eleven**, **twelve**) balls.

How many crayons are there?

There are (**nineteen**, **twenty**) crayons.

How many eggs are there?

There are (**nineteen**, **twenty**) eggs.

Review Test 1

Choose and write.

two three five six butterflies insects animals

1. three puppies

2. ______ goldfish

3. ______ candles

4. ______ ladybugs

5. four ______

6. ______

7. ______

B Circle the correct words.

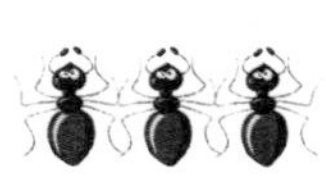
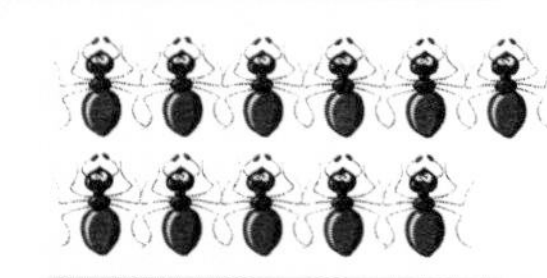

1. three ants + eleven ants = (13, 14) ants

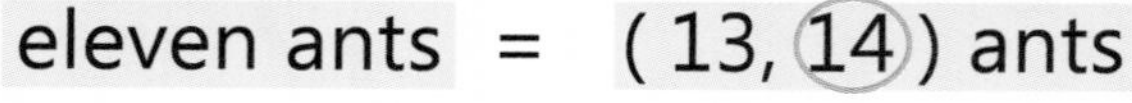
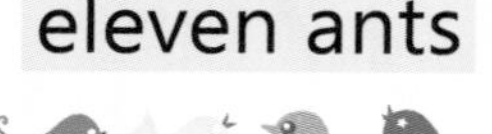

2. six birds + seven birds = (13, 14) birds

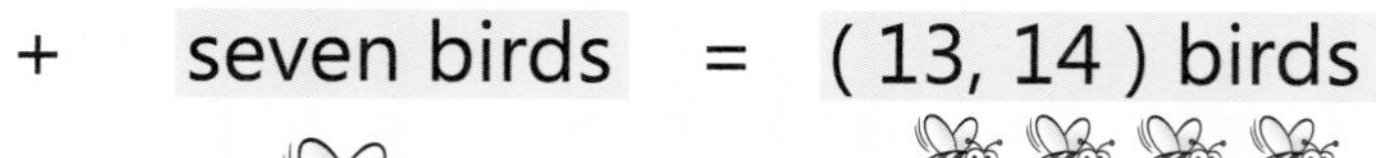

3. eight bees − one bee = (7, 8) bees

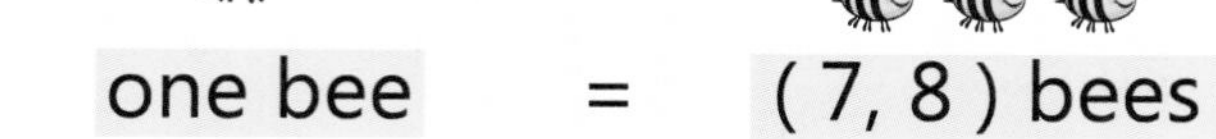

4. nine bees − one bee = (8, 9) bees

C Circle the correct words.

1. How old are you?
   I am (**nine, ten**) years old.

2. How old are you?
   I am (**seven, eight**) years old.

3. I see six butterflies.
   Six is (**one more, one less**) than five.

4. I see eight birds.
   Eight is (**one more, one less**) than nine.

D Match the sentences with the pictures.

1. How many ants are there?
   There are six ants.

2. How many elephants are there?
   There are five elephants.

3. How many pencils are there?
   There are twelve pencils.

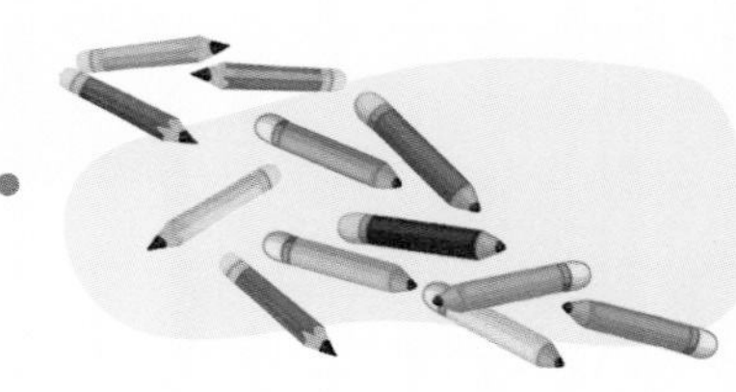

4. How many eggs are there?
   There are twenty eggs.

Numbers from 10 to 100

Key Words

Read the words.

ten 10

twenty 20

thirty 30

forty 40

fifty 50

sixty 60

seventy 70

eighty 80

ninety

one hundred

1 dollar

5 dollars

10 dollars

1 cent

5 cents

10 cents

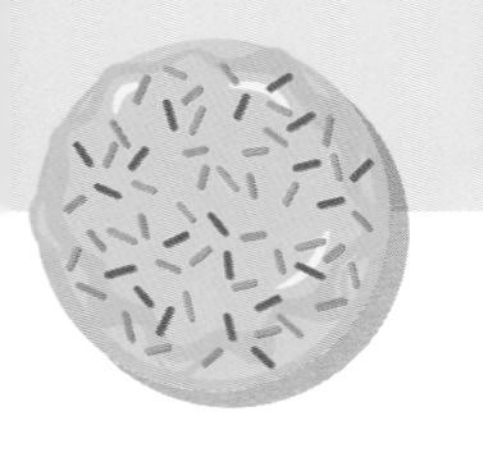

Match the words with the pictures.

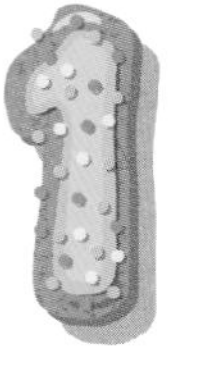

ten

twenty

thirty

forty

fifty

sixty

seventy

eighty

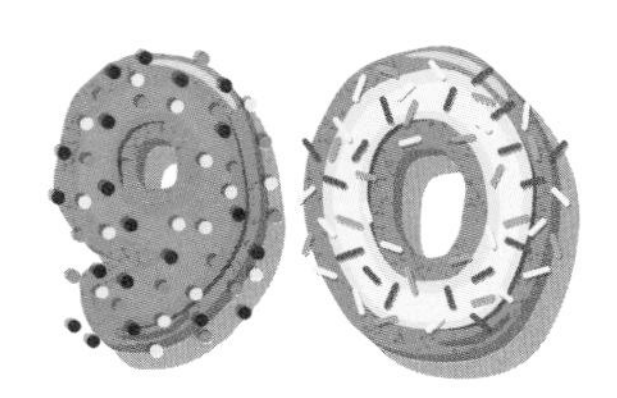

ninety

one hundred

Counting More than 20

Let's Count more than 20. Read the numbers.

twenty-one

twenty-two

twenty-three

twenty-four

25 
twenty-five

twenty-six

27 twenty-seven

twenty-eight

29 twenty-nine

thirty

Circle the words **in blue**.

10 dollars + 10 dollars = (20) dollars

20 dollars + 10 dollars = 30 dollars

30 dollars + 10 dollars = 40 dollars

40 dollars + 10 dollars = 50 dollars

50 dollars + 50 dollars = 100 dollars

How Much Is It?

Underline the words **in blue**.

How much is it?
It is 10 dollars.

How much is it?
It is 25 dollars.

$25.00

$30.05

How much is it?
It is 30 dollars and 5 cents.

$50.20

How much is it?
It's 50 dollars and 20 cents.

$100

How much is it?
It's 100 dollars.

I Can Read

Read the story. Circle the words **in blue**.

Let's Go Shopping.

How much is the doll?

It is 30 dollars and 10 cents.

How much is the cake?

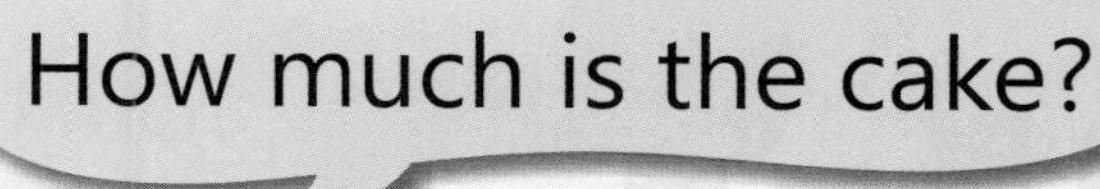

$40.20

It is 40 dollars and 20 cents.

How much is it all together?

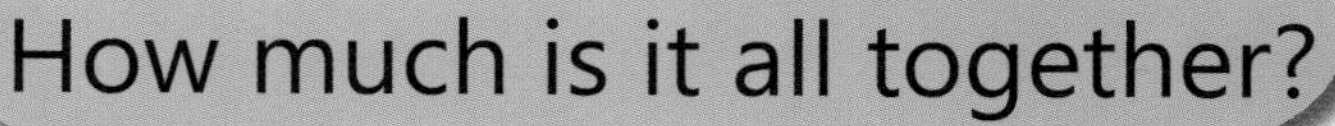

It's 100 dollars and 60 cents all together.

UNIT 6

Numbers from 1st to 10th

Key Words

Read the words.

alphabet

A B C D E

F G H I J

K L M N O

P Q R S T

U V W X y Z

Match Up

Match the words with the pictures.

third

fifth

seventh

eighth

ninth

tenth

What Is First?

Circle the words **in blue**.

A is the first letter of the alphabet.

B is the second letter of the alphabet.

C is the third letter of the alphabet.

D is the fourth letter of the alphabet.

E is the fifth letter of the alphabet.

Which One Is First?

Circle the correct letter for each sentence.

A B C D E F G H I

J K L M N O P Q R

S T U V W X Y Z

Which letter is first?

(**A**, **B**) is the first letter of the alphabet.

Which letter is seventh?

(**G**, **H**) is the seventh letter of the alphabet.

Which letter is tenth?

(**J**, **K**) is the tenth letter of the alphabet.

Which letter is last?

(**Z**, **Y**) is the last letter of the alphabet.

35 Who Is First?

Circle the correct name for each sentence.

 Who is first?

 (Mike, Jane) is first.

 Who is second?

 (Mike, Jane) is second.

 Who is third?

 (Jane, Ann) is third.

 Who is last?

 (Mike, Tom) is last.

I Can Read

Read the story.

Circle the correct word for each sentence.

Where Are They?

Where is Mark?

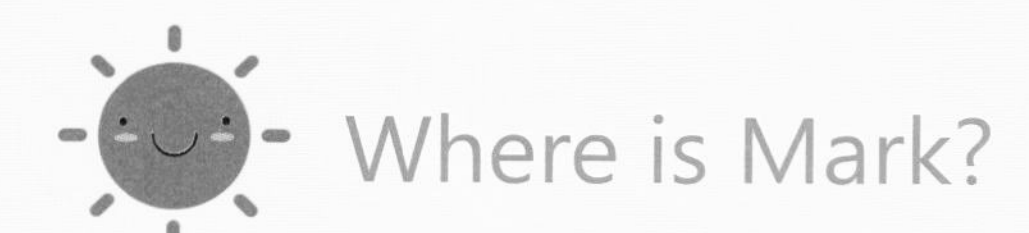

Mark is (**first**, **last**) in line.

Where is Tom?

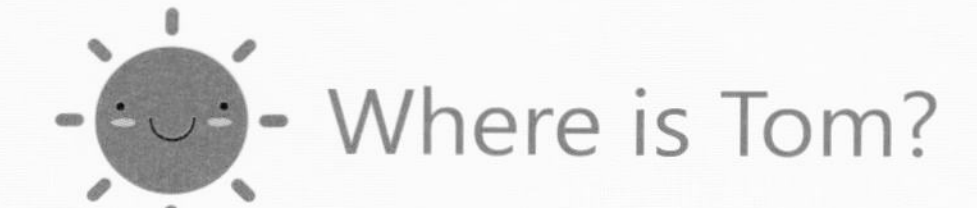

Tom is (**second**, **third**) in line.

Where is Jane?

Jane is (**third, fourth**) in line.

Where is John?

John is (**fifth, sixth**) in line.

Where is Ann?

Ann is (**last, first**) in line.

Time

Key Words Read the words.

1 o'clock

one o'clock

2 o'clock

two o'clock

3 o'clock

three o'clock

4 o'clock

four o'clock

5 o'clock

five o'clock

6 o'clock

six o'clock

7 o'clock

seven o'clock

8 o'clock

eight o'clock

9 o'clock

nine o'clock

10 o'clock

ten o'clock

11 o'clock

eleven o'clock

12 o'clock

twelve o'clock

Match the words with the pictures.

39 What Time Is It?

Circle the correct word for each sentence.

It's (seven, eight) o'clock.

It's (seven, eight) o'clock.

It's (nine, ten) o'clock.

It's (eleven, twelve) o'clock.

It's (eleven, twelve) o'clock.

It's (one, two) o'clock.

What Time Is It?

Circle the correct word for each sentence.

What time is it?
It's (**seven**, **eight**) o'clock.

What time is it?
It's (**seven**, **eight**) o'clock.

What time is it?
It's (**nine**, **ten**) o'clock.

What time is it?
It's (**nine**, **ten**) o'clock.

What time is it?
It's (**eleven**, **twelve**) o'clock.

Circle the words **in blue**.

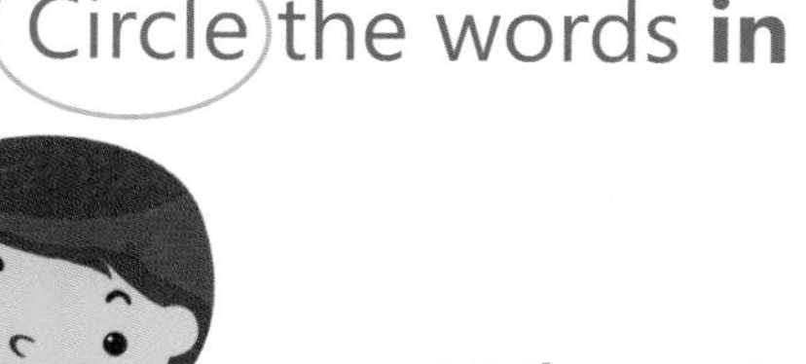

What time is it?

It's twelve ten.

What time is it?

It's one twenty.

What time is it?

It's two thirty.

What time is it?

It's three forty.

What time is it?

It's seven fifty.

I Can Read

Read the story. Circle the words **in blue**.

This Is My Day.

I wake up at 7 o'clock in the morning.

I have breakfast at 8 o'clock.

I go to school at 8:30.

I have lunch at 12 o'clock.

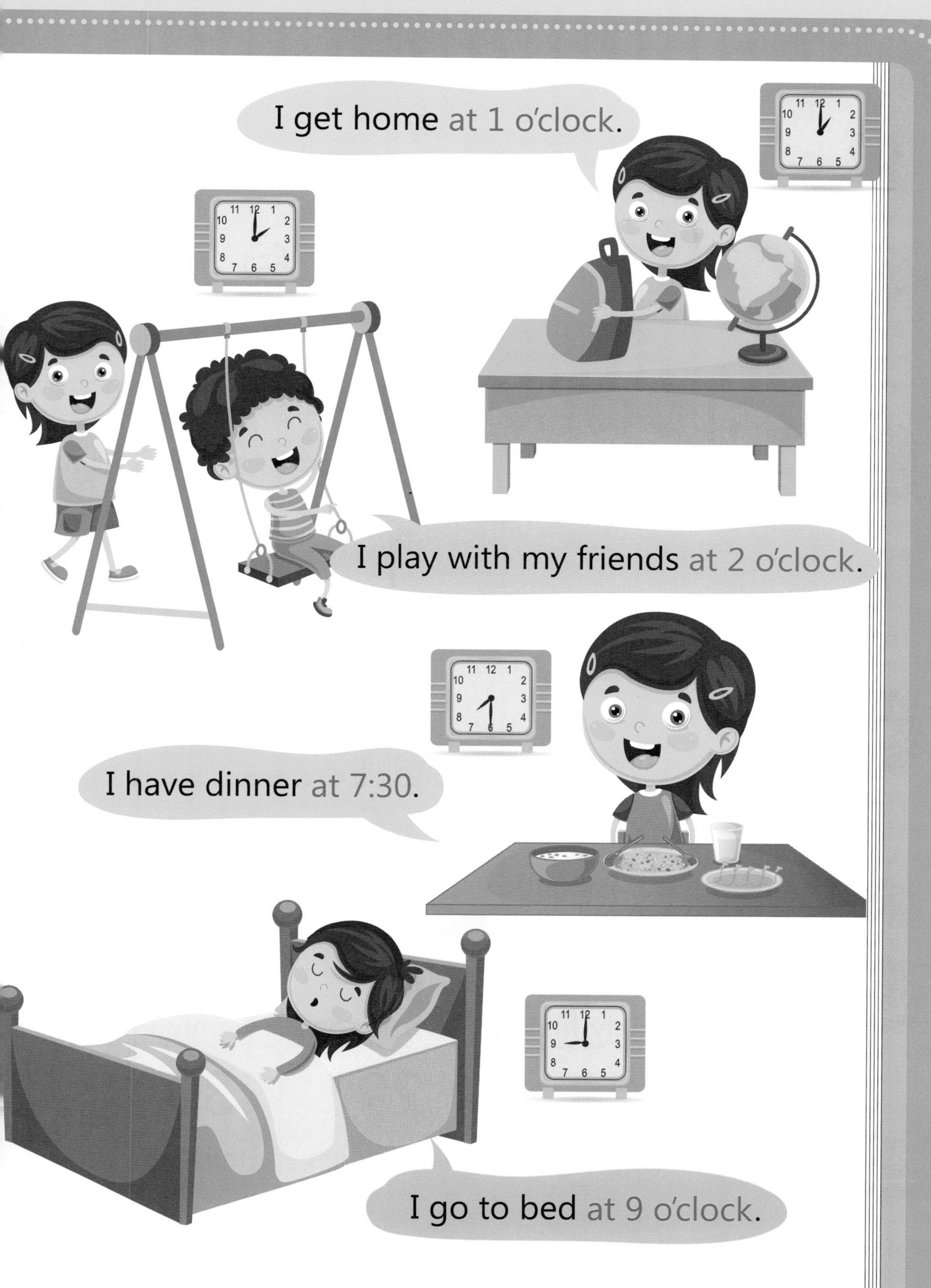
I get home at 1 o'clock.
I play with my friends at 2 o'clock.
I have dinner at 7:30.
I go to bed at 9 o'clock.

UNIT

Reading Calendars

Key Words

Read the word

Calendar

Days — Weeks — Dates — How to read

Sunday	Monday	Tuesday
	1 first	2 second
7 seventh	8 eighth	9 ninth
14 fourteenth	15 fifteenth	16 sixteenth
21 twenty-first	22 twenty-second	23 twenty-third
28 twenty-eighth	29 twenty-ninth	30 thirtieth

Wednesday	Thursday	Friday	Saturday
3 third	4 fourth	5 fifth	6 sixth
10 tenth	11 eleventh	12 twelfth	13 thirteenth
17 seventeenth	18 eighteenth	19 nineteenth	20 twentieth
24 twenty-fourth	25 twenty-fifth	26 twenty-sixth	27 twenty-seventh
31 thirty-first			

Match the words with the pictures.

11th	eleventh	12th
13th	twelfth	14th
15th	thirteenth	21st
22nd	fourteenth	29th
30th	fifteenth	31st
	twenty-first	
	twenty-second	
	twenty-ninth	
	thirtieth	
	thirty-first	

What Day Is It?

Circle the correct word for each sentence.

Sun	Mon	Tue	Wed
1	2 today	3	4
8	9	10	11

What day is it?
It is (Monday, Tuesday).

Sun	Mon	Tue	Wed
1	2	3 today	4
8	9	10	11

What day is it?
It is (**Tuesday, Thursday**).

Tue	Wed	Thu	Fri
3	4 today	5	6
10	11	12	13

What day is it?
It is (**Wednesday, Thursday**).

Tue	Wed	Thu	Fri
3	4	5 today	6
10	11	12	13

What day is it?
It is (**Thursday, Friday**).

Wed	Thu	Fri	Sat
4	5	6 today	7
11	12	13	14

What day is it?
It is (**Friday, Saturday**).

What Date Is It Today?

Read and circle the right date on the calendar.

What date is it today?

It's the eleventh (11th).

What date is it tomorrow?

It's the twelfth (12th).

Sun	Mon	Tue	Wed	Thu	Fri	Sat
1	2	3	4	5	6	7
8	9	10	11 today	12	13	14
15	16	17	18	19	20	21
22	23	24	25	26	27	28
29	30	31				

Sun	Mon	Tue	Wed	Thu	Fri	Sat
1	2	3	4	5	6	7
8	9	10	11	12	13	14
15	16	17	18	19	20	21 today
22	23	24	25	26	27	28
29	30	31				

What date is it today?

It's the twenty-first (21st).

What date is it tomorrow?

It's the twenty-second (22nd).

What Day Is It Today?

Circle the correct word for each sentence.

Today is the 21st.

What day is it today?

It is (**Tuesday, Thursday**).

Tomorrow is the 22nd.

What day is it tomorrow?

It is (**Wednesday, Friday**).

My birthday is the 26th.

What day is it?

It is (**Saturday, Sunday**).

My mom's birthday is the 27th.

What day is it?

It is (**Saturday, Sunday**).

I Can Read

Read the story. Circle the words **in blue**.

Let's Read the Calendar.

There are 7 days in a week.

There are 4 weeks in a month.

There are 12 months in a year.

JANUARY

S	M	T	W	T	F	S
		1	2	3	4	5
6	7	8	9	10	11	12
13	14	15	16	17	18	19
20	21	22	23	24	25	26
27	28	29	30	31		

FEBRUARY

S	M	T	W	T	F	S
					1	2
3	4	5	6	7	8	9
10	11	12	13	14	15	16
17	18	19	20	21	22	23
24	25	26	27	28		

MARCH

S	M	T	W	T	F	S
					1	2
3	4	5	6	7	8	9
10	11	12	13	14	15	16
17	18	19	20	21	22	23
24	25	26	27	28	29	30
31						

JULY

S	M	T	W	T	F	S
	1	2	3	4	5	6
7	8	9	10	11	12	13
14	15	16	17	18	19	20
21	22	23	24	25	26	27
28	29	30	31			

AUGUST

S	M	T	W	T	F	S
				1	2	3
4	5	6	7	8	9	10
11	12	13	14	15	16	17
18	19	20	21	22	23	24
25	26	27	28	29	30	31

SEPTEMBER

S	M	T	W	T	F	S
1	2	3	4	5	6	7
8	9	10	11	12	13	14
15	16	17	18	19	20	21
22	23	24	25	26	27	28
29	30					

There are 365 days in a year.

And there are 24 hours in one day.

APRIL

S	M	T	W	T	F	S
	1	2	3	4	5	6
7	8	9	10	11	12	13
14	15	16	17	18	19	20
21	22	23	24	25	26	27
28	29	30				

MAY

S	M	T	W	T	F	S
			1	2	3	4
5	6	7	8	9	10	11
12	13	14	15	16	17	18
19	20	21	22	23	24	25
26	27	28	29	30	31	

JUNE

S	M	T	W	T	F	S
						1
2	3	4	5	6	7	8
9	10	11	12	13	14	15
16	17	18	19	20	21	22
23	24	25	26	27	28	29
30						

OCTOBER

S	M	T	W	T	F	S
		1	2	3	4	5
6	7	8	9	10	11	12
13	14	15	16	17	18	19
20	21	22	23	24	25	26
27	28	29	30	31		

NOVEMBER

S	M	T	W	T	F	S
					1	2
3	4	5	6	7	8	9
10	11	12	13	14	15	16
17	18	19	20	21	22	23
24	25	26	27	28	29	30

DECEMBER

S	M	T	W	T	F	S
1	2	3	4	5	6	7
8	9	10	11	12	13	14
15	16	17	18	19	20	21
22	23	24	25	26	27	28
29	30	31				

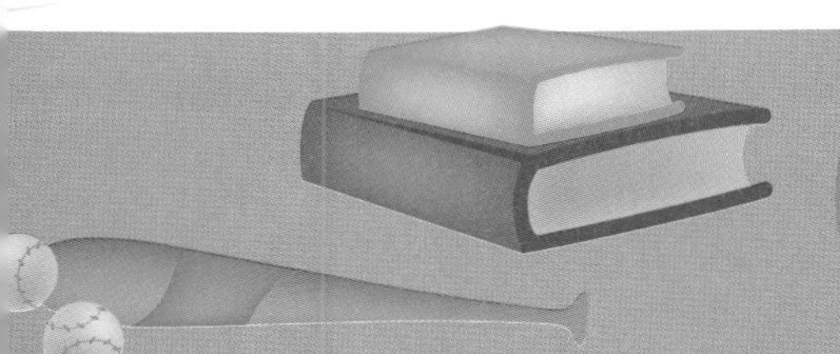

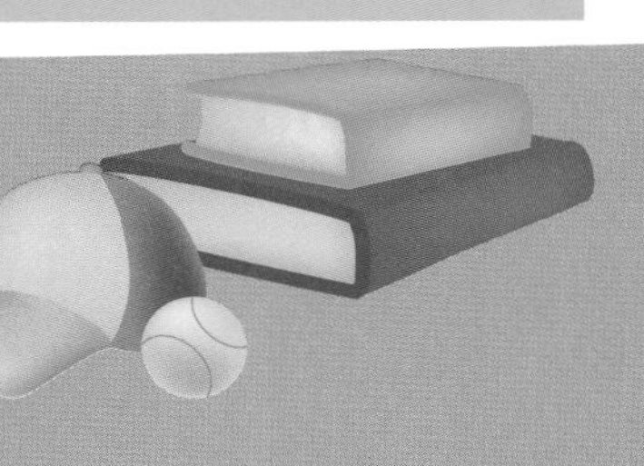

Review Test 2

A Choose and write.

thirty forty fifty one hundred days alphabet dates

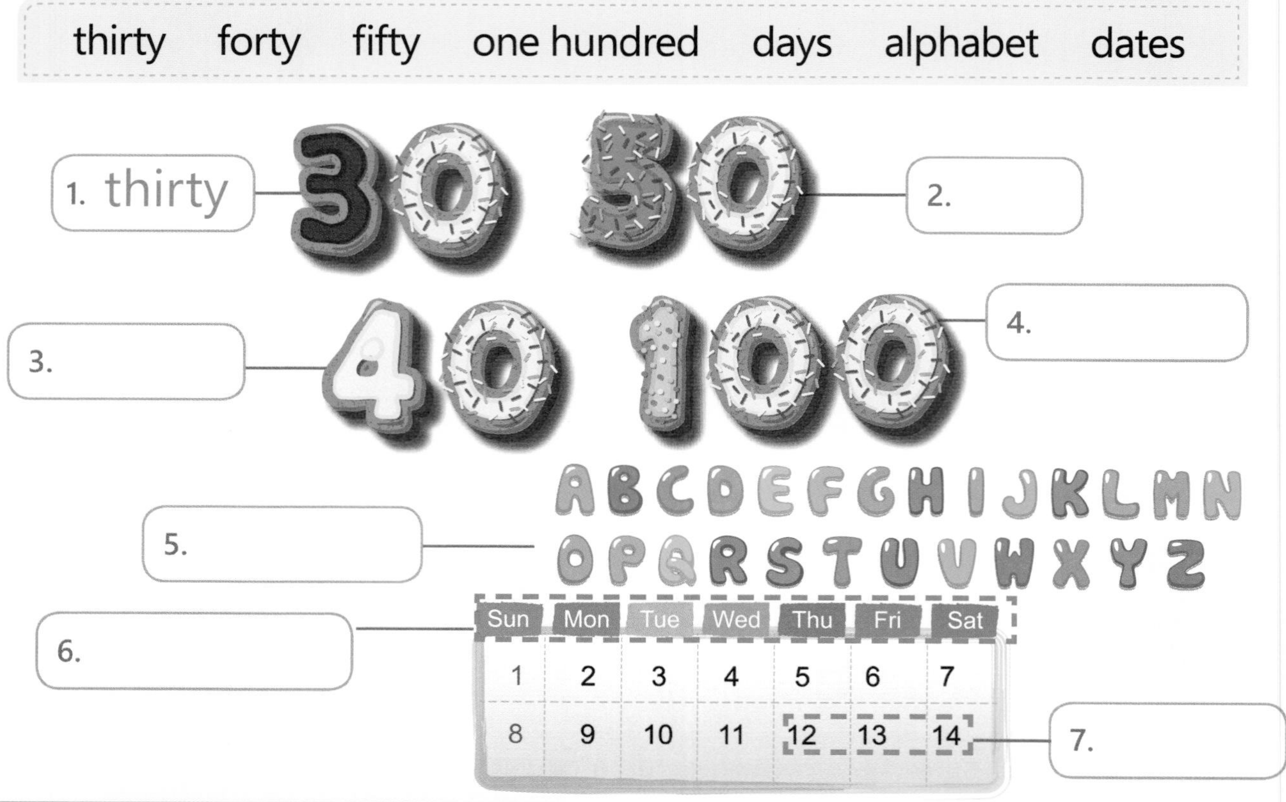

B Circle the correct words.

1. **A** is the (**first, second**) letter of the alphabet.

2. **Z** is the (**last, third**) letter of the alphabet.

3. Jane is (**third, fourth**) in line.

4. Tom is (**second, third**) in line.

 C Circle the correct words.

1. What time is it?
   It's (**seven**, **eight**) o'clock.

2. What time is it?
   It's (**eleven**, **twelve**) ten.

3. How much is the cap?
   It's 20 (**dollars**, **cents**).

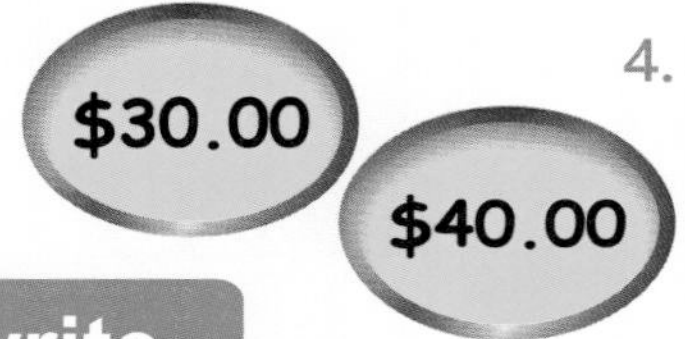

4. How much is it all together?
   It's (**70**, **80**) dollars all together.

 D Answer and write.

eleventh   Thursday   Friday   twenty-first

Wed	Thu	Fri	Sat
4	5 today	6	7
11	12	13	14

1. What day is it today?
   It is Thursday.

2. What day is it tomorrow?
   It is ________.

Wed	Thu	Fri	Sat
4	5 today	6	7
11	12	13	14

3. What date is it today?
   It's the ________.

4. What date is it today?
   It's the ________.

Unit 1

Numbers from 1 to 5
數字：從 1 到 5

1. **one** 一；一個
2. **two** 二；兩個
3. **three** 三；三個
4. **four** 四；四個
5. **five** 五；五個
6. **cat** 貓
7. **kitten** 小貓
8. **dog** 狗
9. **puppy** 小狗
10. **goldfish** 金魚
11. **bird** 小鳥
12. **There is** 有（單數）
13. **There are** 有（複數）
14. **two kittens** 兩隻小貓
15. **three puppies** 三隻小狗
16. **four birds** 四隻小鳥
17. **five goldfish** 五隻金魚
18. **I have** 我有
19. **How many . . .** 多少……
20. **How many cats are there?** 有幾隻貓？

Unit 2

Numbers from 6 to 10
數字：從 6 到 10

1. **six** 六；六個
2. **seven** 七；七個
3. **eight** 八；八個
4. **nine** 九；九個
5. **ten** 十；十個
6. **candle** 蠟燭
7. **present** 禮物
8. **birthday cake** 生日蛋糕
9. **cupcake** 杯子蛋糕
10. **balloon** 氣球

11 **I am . . .** 我是……

12 **6 years old** 六歲

13 **7 years old** 七歲

14 **8 years old** 八歲

15 **9 years old** 九歲

16 **10 years old** 十歲

17 **How old are you?** 你幾歲？

18 **I am ten years old.** 我十歲。

19 **Happy birthday!** 生日快樂！

20 **Let's . . .** 讓我們……

21 **have a party** 舉辦派對

Unit 3

One More, One Less

多一個，少一個

1 **ant** 螞蟻

2 **ants** 螞蟻們

3 **butterfly** 蝴蝶

4 **butterflies** 蝴蝶們

5 **ladybug** 瓢蟲

6 **ladybugs** 瓢蟲們

7 **bee** 蜜蜂

8 **bees** 蜜蜂們

9 **plus** 加

10 **minus** 減

11 **equal** 等於

12 **one more** 多一個

13 **one less** 少一個

14 **one more than** 比……多一個

15 **one less than** 比……少一個

16 **I see . . .** 我看到……

17 **I see six butterflies.**
我看到六隻蝴蝶。

Unit 4

Numbers from 11 to 20

數字：從 11 到 20

1 **eleven** 十一；十一個

2 **twelve** 十二；十二個

3 **thirteen** 十三；十三個

4 **fourteen** 十四；十四個

5 **fifteen** 十五；十五個

6 **sixteen** 十六；十六個

7 **seventeen** 十七；十七個

8 **eighteen** 十八；十八個

9 **nineteen** 十九；十九個

10 **twenty** 二十；二十個

11 **animal** 動物

12 **lion** 獅子

13 **tiger** 老虎

14 **elephant** 大象

15 **insect** 昆蟲

16 **row** 列；排

17 **in row 1** 在第一排

18 **in row 2** 在第二排

19 **in row 3** 在第三排

20 **all together** 總共

21 **count** 計算

22 **Let's count.** 讓我們來計算吧！

23 **pencil** 鉛筆

24 **ball** 球

25 **crayon** 蠟筆

26 **egg** 蛋

Unit 5

Numbers from 10 to 100
數字：從10到100

1 **ten** 十；十個

2 **twenty** 二十；二十個

3 **thirty** 三十；三十個

4 **forty** 四十；四十個

5 **fifty** 五十；五十個

6 **sixty** 六十；六十個

7 **seventy** 七十；七十個

8 **eighty** 八十；八十個

9 **ninety** 九十；九十個

10 **one hundred** 一百；一百個

11 **1 dollar** 一塊錢

12 **5 dollars** 五塊錢

13 **10 dollars** 十塊錢

14 **1 cent** 一分錢

15 **5 cents** 五分錢

16 **10 cents** 十分錢

17 **Let's count more than 20.**
讓我們數到二十以上。

18 **Read the numbers.**
閱讀這些數字。

19 **twenty-one** 二十一；二十一個

20 **twenty-two** 二十二；二十二個

21 **twenty-three** 二十三；二十三個

22 **twenty-four** 二十四；二十四個

23 **twenty-five** 二十五；二十五個

24 **twenty-six** 二十六；二十六個

25 **twenty-seven** 二十七；二十七個

26 **twenty-eight** 二十八；二十八個

27 **twenty-nine** 二十九；二十九個

28 **thirty** 三十；三十個

29 **How much is it?** 它多少錢？

30 **20 dollars** 二十塊錢

31 **30 dollars** 三十塊錢

32 **40 dollars** 四十塊錢

33 **50 dollars** 五十塊錢

34 **100 dollars** 一百塊錢

35 **go shopping** 去購物

36 **book** 書本

37 **cap** 鴨舌帽

38 **doll** 洋娃娃

39 **cake** 蛋糕

Unit 6

Numbers from 1st to 10th
序數：從第一到第十

1 **first** 第一個；第一的

2 **second** 第二個；第二的

3 **third** 第三個；第三的

4 **fourth** 第四個；第四的

5 **fifth** 第五個；第五的

6 **sixth** 第六個；第六的

7 **seventh** 第七個；第七的

8 **eighth** 第八個；第八的

9 **ninth** 第九個；第九的

10 **tenth** 第十個；第十個

11 **last** 最後一個；最後的

12 **alphabet** 字母表

13 **What is first?** 第一個是什麼？

14 **letter** 字母

15 **the first letter** 第一個字母

16 **the second letter** 第二個字母

17 **the third letter** 第三個字母

18 **the fourth letter** 第四個字母

19 **the fifth letter** 第五個字母

20 **Which one is first?**
哪一個是第一個？

21 **which letter** 哪個字母

22 **Who is first?** 誰是第一個？

23 **Who is second?** 誰是第二個？

24 **Who is third?** 誰是第三個？

25 **Who is last?** 誰是最後一個？

26 **Where are they?** 它們在哪裡？

27 **Where is Mark?** 馬克在哪裡？

Unit 7

Time
時間

1 **1 o'clock** 一點鐘

2 **2 o'clock** 兩點鐘

3 **3 o'clock** 三點鐘

4 **4 o'clock** 四點鐘

5 **5 o'clock** 五點鐘

6 **6 o'clock** 六點鐘

7 **7 o'clock** 七點鐘

8 **8 o'clock** 八點鐘

9 **9 o'clock** 九點鐘

10 **10 o'clock** 十點鐘

11 **11 o'clock** 十一點鐘

12 **12 o'clock** 十二點鐘

13 **What time is it?** 現在幾點？

14 **It's seven o'clock.** 現在是七點鐘。

15 **It's twelve ten.** 現在是 12 點 10 分。

16 **It's one twenty.** 現在是 1 點 20 分。

17 **It's two thirty.** 現在是 2 點 30 分。

18 **It's three forty.** 現在是 3 點 40 分。

19 **It's seven fifty.** 現在是 7 點 50 分。

20 **wake up** 起床

21 **at 7 o'clock** 在七點整

22 **in the morning** 在早上

23 **have breakfast** 吃早餐

24 **go to school** 去上學

25 **have lunch** 吃午餐

26 **get home** 抵達家裡

27 **play with my friends** 和我的朋友玩

28 **have dinner** 吃晚餐

29 **go to bed** 上床睡覺

Unit 8

Reading Calendars
閱讀月曆

1 **calendar** 月曆

2 **days** 星期

3 **weeks** 週

4 **dates** 日子；日期

5 **how to read** 如何閱讀

6 **Sunday** 星期日

7 **Monday** 星期一

8 **Tuesday** 星期二

9 **Wednesday** 星期三

10 **Thursday** 星期四

11 **Friday** 星期五

12 **Saturday** 星期六

Sunday	Monday	Tuesday	Wednesday	Thursday	Friday	Saturday
	1 **1st** 一號	2 **2nd** 二號	3 **3rd** 三號	4 **4th** 四號	5 **5th** 五號	6 **6th** 六號
7 **7th** 七號	8 **8th** 八號	9 **9th** 九號	10 **10th** 十號	11 **11th** 十一號	12 **12th** 十二號	13 **13th** 十三號
14 **14th** 十四號	15 **15th** 十五號	16 **16th** 十六號	17 **17th** 十七號	18 **18th** 十八號	19 **19th** 十九號	20 **20th** 二十號
21 **21st** 二十一號	22 **22nd** 二十二號	23 **23rd** 二十三號	24 **24th** 二十四號	25 **25th** 二十五號	26 **26th** 二十六號	27 **27th** 二十七號
28 **28th** 二十八號	29 **29th** 二十九號	30 **30th** 三十號	31 **31st** 三十一號			

13 **What day is it?** 今天星期幾？

14 **It is Monday.** 今天是星期一。

15 **today** 今天

16 **tomorrow** 明天

17 **What date is it today?**
今天幾號？

18 **It's the eleventh (11th).**
今天是十一號。

19 **my birthday** 我的生日

20 **my mom's birthday** 我媽媽的生日

21 **7 days** 7 天

22 **4 weeks** 4 個禮拜

23 **12 months** 12 個月

24 **365 days** 365 天

25 **24 hours** 24 小時

26 **in a week** 一個禮拜裡

27 **in a month** 一個月裡

28 **in a year** 一年裡

29 **in one day** 一天裡

國家圖書館出版品預行編目資料

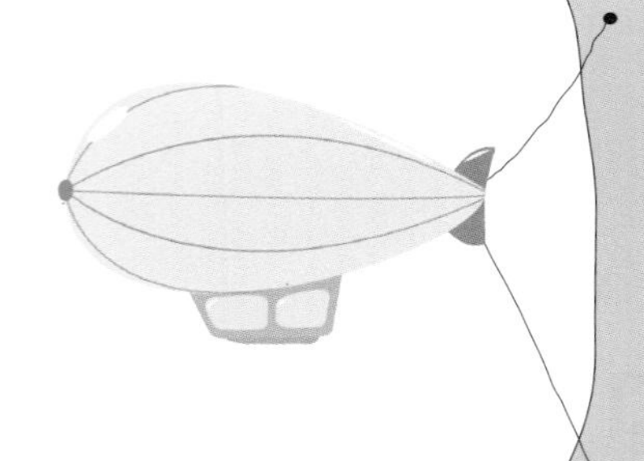

Fun 學美國各學科 Preschool 閱讀課本 . 6，數字篇 / Michael A. Putlack, e-Creative Contents 著 ; 歐寶妮譯 . -- 二版 . -- [臺北市] : 寂天文化， 2018.12
面 ; 公分

ISBN 978-986-318-766-0 (平裝附光碟片)

1. 英語 2. 詞彙
805.12 107022017

FUN學美國各學科 Preschool 閱讀課本 6 數字篇 二版

作　　者　Michael A. Putlack & e-Creative Contents
譯　　者　歐寶妮
編　　輯　賴祖兒／歐寶妮
主　　編　丁宥暄
內文排版　洪伊珊
封面設計　林書玉
製程管理　洪巧玲
出 版 者　寂天文化事業股份有限公司
電　　話　02-2365-9739
傳　　真　02-2365-9835
網　　址　www.icosmos.com.tw
讀者服務　onlineservice@icosmos.com.tw
出版日期　2018 年 12 月　二版一刷　080201

郵撥帳號　1998620-0　寂天文化事業股份有限公司
劃撥金額 600（含）元以上者，郵資免費。
訂購金額 600 元以下者，加收 65 元運費。
〔若有破損，請寄回更換，謝謝〕